I0578779

THE BLOOD PACT

RITE WORLD 9: RITE OF THE WOLF

JULIANA HAYGERT

COPYRIGHT

This book is a work of fiction. Names, characters, places, and incidents either are products of the author's imagination or are used fictitiously. Any resemblance to actual persons, living or dead, events, or locales is entirely coincidental.

Copyright © 2020 by Juliana Haygert

All rights reserved. This book or any portion thereof may not be reproduced or used in any manner whatsoever without the express written permission of the publisher except for the use of brief quotations in a book review.

Manufactured in the United States of America.

First Edition September 2020

www.JulianaHaygert.com

Cover design by Moonchildljilja

Any trademark, service marks, product names, or names featured are the property of their respective owners, and are used only for reference. There is no implied endorsement if one of these terms is used.

❀ Created with Vellum

AUTHOR'S NOTE

I hope you enjoy reading *The Blood Pact*!

Don't forget to sign up for my Newsletter to find out about new releases, cover reveals, giveaways, and more!

If you want to see exclusive teasers, help me decide on covers, read excerpts, talk about books, etc, join my reader group on Facebook: Juliana's Club!

RITE WORLD

Welcome to the RITE WORLD!

Free Novella:
The Vampire Hunt

Rite World:
The Vampire Heir (Book 1)
The Witch Queen (Book 2)
The Immortal Vow (Book 3)
The Warlock Lord (Book 4)
The Wolf Consort (Book 5)
The Crystal Rose (Book 6)
The Wolf Forsaken (Book 7)
The Fae Bound (Book 8)
The Blood Pact (Book 9)

Rite World: Blackthorn Hunters Academy
The Demons Kiss (Book 1)

The Hunter Secret (Book 2)
The Soul Bond (Book 3)
The Shadow Trials (Book 4)
The Immortal Vow (Book 5)

And more to come!

THE VAMPIRE HUNT

I have an exclusive novella set in the Rite World that is just for my newsletter subscribers!

Click here to sign-up and receive your book!

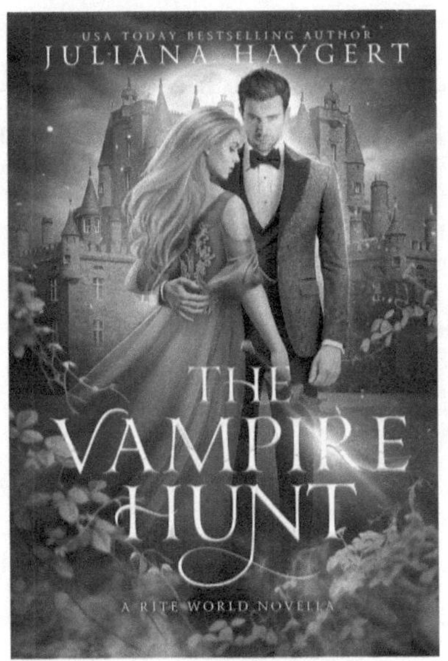

THE VAMPIRE HUNT
A Rite World Novella

Norah is a demon hunter, one of the best graduated from the Blackthorn Hunters Academy. When she's sent to investigate a case concerning demons in a small town, she runs into a very arrogant vampire. Her first instinct is to kill him, after all, he's a supernatural and demon hunters are taught to end all evil.

Cain is a vampire prince. Because of his status, he's in charge of making sure humans don't find out about his kind. During a routine investigation, he bumps into a very sexy demon hunter and he wonders what she's doing on his way.

However, the case grows much bigger for Norah and Cain to handle alone. To find the truth and win this battle, the vampire and the demon hunter will have to hunt together —without killing each other.

How well could this end?

1

FARRAH

I DIDN'T HAVE TO LOOK FOR THEM. THEY CAME TO ME.

Not even fifteen minutes after I left Starlight Vale behind, Myra and two other witches stepped in my way. They raised their hands, their magic at their fingertips. With the frost pendant, I didn't think they could win if we were to battle.

But I wasn't here to battle.

I lifted my arms above my head. "I won't fight you."

Myra cocked an eyebrow at me. I hadn't seen her in three years, and the last time we had been in the same room, she had been torturing me, preparing me for the sacrifice they wanted.

I hated her almost as much as I hated the Queen of the Bonecrown witches.

She didn't relax. "Then what are you doing?"

"I'm not going to resist it," I told her, my voice flat, my face emotionless. "Take me to Corvina. I have a deal for her."

<hr>

HOURS LATER, WE ARRIVED AT THE ROCKY HILL FORMING THE base of a mountain. I paused and looked up, northward. I had come this way before, with Wyatt, Luana, and Keeran. I had brought them here right after they rescued me from these dark witches. Luana and Keeran had gone further, while Wyatt had stayed behind with me, because I was too afraid of the witches.

I wasn't afraid now.

Myra glanced over her shoulder. "Do I have to go get you?"

I let out a long breath. "No." I followed her into the Bonecrown territory.

Instantly, the sky darkened some more. Soon, we walked over a smooth white stone path that led up the mountainside, hundreds of bones flanking it.

As we went up the mountain, mist clouded the way.

Half a mile up the mountain, the path opened to a plateau. Dozens of houses stood close together, and behind them, a black castle—not as big as the shadow fae king's, but still very intimidating.

We strolled through the main road into town, toward the castle. Several witches spied on us from their windows. Some came out and snickered at me, as if I was a disgusting bug that needed to be squashed. Did they all remember me? Did they all want to rip my throat out right now?

Even though the warlocks had been out in the world for three years now, I didn't see one man among the witches. They were still probably following their old traditions—imprisoning human men and using them as slaves.

In the castle, we walked across a dark foyer and an archway into the main hall—a narrow room with sleek black stone flooring, and at the end, a large throne made entirely of bones.

Corvina, the queen of the Bonecrown witches, was seated on it.

Upon seeing me, a wide smile spread over her lips.

"My oh my, what do we have here?" She stood up, her elegant black dress full around her. Her black hair was pulled down on her back, dark makeup was smeared over her face, and a heavy crown made of bones was on top of her head. "Dear Farrah. When you surrendered to the shadow fae prince, I didn't think I would see you anymore." Her thick eyebrows curled down. "But I hear you killed him."

I raised my chin, showing her I wasn't the same girl as before. I wasn't afraid of her. Actually, I was just as powerful as she was. "I did," I said. "But because of that, the fae king is here on Earth."

The smile left Corvina's lips. "That fae king ..." Something coursed through her body, almost like a shudder. Was she disgusted by him, or was she afraid? Interesting.

"I came here to make a deal," I continued.

She stared at me. "A deal? My dear, you just walked into my castle. I can now simply get a hold of you and finally use you for my sacrifice."

I inhaled, calling on my magic. It was so abundant, I

was sure she could feel it from where she stood. "I would like to see you try."

Her sly smile was back. "My oh my, someone grew up into a fierce woman. I like it."

"Will you hear me out or not?"

Seeming bored, Corvina waved a hand at me. "Go on."

"I'm stronger now, and I'm pretty sure I can at least fight my way out of here," I started. Being stronger was always the problem here. She wanted me for my power. Now that I was even more powerful, she probably wanted me even more. "But I won't, if you accept my deal. I'll stay and serve as your sacrifice, willingly, if you help me bring the shadow fae king down first."

Her dark eyes narrowed. She considered it for a minute. I was sure she didn't like the idea of having the fae king in the human realm. He was too close for comfort, and he was purely evil. He would soon rage war against not just the fae, but all supernaturals, including witches.

It was in her interest—in all of our interest—to have the fae king gone.

The seconds ticked by, and I fought not to squirm under her intense stare.

"If you don't agree," I said, starting to get too uncomfortable about this. "I won't let you have me. I'll fight my way out of here, and if I can't escape, I'll kill myself so you can't use me as you intend to."

Corvina didn't flinch. For a full minute, she didn't even move. She just stared at me, as if she could see something I was hiding inside my head.

Then she finally said, "I need time to consider this."

2

I COULDN'T BELIEVE SHE HAD LEFT ME LIKE THIS.

Again.

What the fuck?

This time I wasn't desperate, or worried, though. I was fucking pissed. Why was her excuse now? She was going to turn herself to the fae king? Hadn't we already established that wouldn't work at all?

After getting dressed and washing up, I stomped out of my bedroom and into the communal area in between the guests' buildings. Thankfully, not many people were awake or out at this time of the morning, but the ones that mattered were here: Daleigh, Ariella, and Kayden. The trio was seated at one end of a long table, tea mugs in front of them.

They saw me approaching with easy demeanor, but when I got close, they noticed something was amiss and tension spread through the group.

"What's wrong?" Ariella was the first to ask.

"Farrah left," I told them.

Daleigh shot up. "What? What do you mean?"

I shrugged. "I woke up and she was gone." Again, I almost said out loud, but shut my lips tight. Ariella might remember that, but the others didn't need to know.

Ariella blanched. "You don't think she went to the fae king?"

I shook my head. "Why would she have left just to go back there? There's something else going on, I just can't pinpoint what."

"We should go after her," Kayden said, standing up. "She can't have gotten far."

I nodded, though I had been asleep most of the night. She could have left hours earlier and be very far away. Still, I couldn't stop having hope. I wished I would step outside and find her there, frozen in place, unsure about leaving, considering coming back to me. I would hold her hand and tell her to stay.

Where the fuck had she gone?

We agreed to pack small bags and meet at the front gates of Starlight Vale in fifteen minutes. I was in my room, shoving some spare change of clothes in my bag when there was a knock on the door. A moment later, Luana stepped in.

"What are you doing?" she asked, her eyes on the bag over the bed. "You're leaving?"

I let out a sigh. "I'm going after Farrah."

Luana frowned. "What do you mean?"

I told her about Farrah just upping and leaving, and that it wasn't the first time she did that. If I knew Farrah, she was up to no good, and I had to find her before she did something that she would regret.

After a tense silence, Luana crossed her arms and nodded. "Go. Find her. But then come back here. We'll keep an eye on the fae king. If he tries anything, we'll stop him, but Wyatt ... from what I've seen, from what I've felt, I'm not sure we can defeat them so easily. We might need help. All the help we can get."

"I know," I whispered. Defeating the shadow fae king before he stepped foot outside his new castle was a priority, of course, but I couldn't just focus on that and forget about Farrah. Besides, Farrah was fucking powerful. We needed her here, helping us. I turned to Luana. "I'll be back soon, I promise."

Luana clasped a hand over my shoulder. "Take care."

DALEIGH, ARIELLA, KAYDEN, AND I LEFT STARLIGHT VALE and started our journey through the forest, trying to track where Farrah might have gone. But there was no clue, no track. There was no way of knowing which direction she had gone.

At some point, we separated and went different ways, trying to find something, anything that served as a clue. But Farrah wasn't stupid. If she didn't want to be found, she would have been careful not to leave anything behind.

After a couple of hours, the trio and I met again beside a stream that cut through the forest.

"We can't continue blind like this," Kayden said, obviously bored with the search, and irritated because things weren't going the way we first agreed. "If we can't find her, then we should go back to Starlight Vale and help the others with the fae king."

"The fae king is quiet for now," Daleigh said. "He scared us away, but didn't chase us."

"For now," she rebuked. "I'm sure he won't just glare at us from his dark castle for long."

"Isn't there a fae way of tracking?" I asked. Like the others, I was frustrated about the way things were developing.

"No," Daleigh snapped. "How about that werewolf nose of yours? Can't you pick up her scent?"

She was my fucking mate and I hadn't caught one single whiff in the forest. Sure I would shout some angry words if I opened my mouth, I just shook my head.

Then I froze. I heard faint shuffling before the scent of decay reached my nose. "Shhh," I told the others in a whisper. "We're not alone."

Two seconds later, dark figures lunged for us. If I hadn't smelled them, I would have thought it was shadow fae coming for us. But these were demons—Drollmor's demons—and they were here for me.

We didn't wait for it. The moment the demons appeared, I shifted to my demon wolf and we lunged at them. With the four of us, it didn't take long for the demons to fall. I alone killed four of them in less than ten seconds. With their powers, the others fared just as well.

After the fight was done and bloody bodies littered the forest ground, I shifted back and quickly put on a spare pair of pants and shirt and shoes, but I stayed back, sensing the heat of her gaze from across the stream.

Ariella couldn't help herself. "They came for you."

Daleigh frowned. "What do you mean?"

"Wyatt sold his soul to a higher demon and now said demon wants his due," she said, no hesitation. Just anger.

Daleigh turned his blue eyes at me. "You did what?"

I groaned. "I fucked up and I don't want to talk about that." I gestured toward the demons at our feet. "They are dead."

"But more will come," Kayden said, her tone flat. Ariella nodded in agreement.

I gritted my teeth. "I would love to just meet Drollmor and kill the fucking demon, but right now, finding Farrah is more important."

At that, Ariella's gray eyes changed, and her shoulder sagged. "I ..." She inhaled deeply. "I think I can help with that."

I stared at her. "What are you talking about?"

She pointed to the body right in front of her. "I know of a spell, a dark magic spell, that uses demon blood to track supernatural beings. Normally, I would say it wouldn't work with a fae, but if I get a drop of blood from Daleigh, and use your connection to her to—"

Daleigh snapped his head between us. "Connection?"

I frowned. "You haven't figured out yet?"

Daleigh's face paled. "You're her mate?"

I didn't say anything. I just stared at him. I wouldn't argue about this. There was nothing he, or anyone for that matter, could do to change the mating bond.

"Are you sure you want to do that?" Kayden asked, since no one else did. I felt bad for Ariella. She was an angel, a fallen angel whose soul could be easily corrupted, and now she would use dark magic to help me. But I was just that selfish. I wanted this to work. I needed this to work.

Ariella nodded. "It's the only way."

Swiftly, Ariella got a drop of blood from Daleigh, and some other things, and started the spell. She closed her eyes and pressed a hand to my chest. As she chanted, I felt something stirring, warming.

Ariella's arm shook and her eyelids trembled. I thought she was going to pass out, but suddenly she opened her eyes and stared at me. "I know where she is."

3

———————

FARRAH

SEATED AT THE FRONT STONE STEPS OF THE MANOR, I PETTED Rusty, who was tucked on my side. The damn cat had shown up last night, after Myra had shown me this house, hidden in path halfway down the mountain, and nestled in a clearing beside a cliff. She had told me this was where Luana and Keeran had stayed when they visited them over three years ago.

In the middle of the night, a servant might have come, because now the kitchen was stocked up, and there were fresh linen and towels on the foyer's table, among other things.

Despite knowing where I was and with whom, I had slept well and I was comfortable here.

And now I waited until Corvina came to me to tell me her decision.

It was late in the morning when Myra appeared at the manor. "Come with me," she said, stoic as ever.

Knowing I better not give them a reason to turn down

my deal, I promptly stood up. The cat jumped from the steps and disappeared inside the manor.

In silence, I followed Myra up the mountain, through the same path we had taken the previous day. But instead of taking me to the main castle, she veered left and took me through a lush green garden with many thick bushes, and ivy covered benches and archways.

The garden opened up in a clearing of sorts, with a round stone flooring. Corvina, wearing another elegant black gown, stood in the center, in front of a stone pedestal that reached to her waist. On top of the pedestal was a silver bowl.

I frowned, my eyes on the bowl, as I approached her. "What's that for?"

"Well, my dear, I hope you're not stupid enough to think I'll make a deal with you just trusting your words," she said, matter-of-factly. I started. What? She was going to accept it? "Before I come to a decision, I need to be sure of your true intentions." Corvina picked up a long needle from beside the bowl and handed it to me. "Prick your finger and let a few drops of your blood in the bowl."

I didn't like this, but I understood where she was coming from. Witches didn't trust easily, especially this coven. Corvina wouldn't lie in bed with me without guarantees.

Bracing myself for whatever spell she was going to perform, I took the needled from her, pierced my index finger. Blood pooled against my fair skin. I turned my hand to the bowl and let a couple of drops down.

"Is that enough?" I asked, pulling my hand back.

Corvina nodded. Myra handed me a small white towel. I pressed the towel to my finger.

Closing her eyes, Corvina stretched her hand forward, hovering it over the bowl. A minute later, her eyes snapped open and she glared at me. "I knew it." She shook her head. "Your heart is compromised. You love a werewolf and if he's put in danger, you'll back out of the deal."

"I—"

"Don't try to fool me," she said, cutting me off. "I've seen it all. During a battle, he'll get hurt and you'll save him, at the cost of your own life, thus rendering our deal null."

I opened my mouth to argue but shut it again. I didn't know how she could see the future, but she was right. If Wyatt ever got hurt and I was able to fix it by laying down my life, then it was true. Wasn't I doing that right now? Just I wasn't trying to save only him. I was trying to save them all. I had to hold on to that thought. "I won't back down—"

"I know you think won't, but you won't be *thinking*." She shook her head again. "I won't make a deal with you ..." She paused, almost giving me a heart attack in anticipation. "Unless you make a blood pact with me."

I sucked in a sharp breath. Of course she would go that far. She was the damn queen of the darkest witches of all. But I had no choice. It was this, or she wouldn't help me. "I'll do it."

In a flash, Corvina shot forward. With a wicked smile, she grabbed my wrist and turned my hand, my palm up. Myra handed her a silver dagger. She ran the tip of the blade across my palm. I hissed as the pain spread through my hand. Then she did it with her own hand.

She pressed her palm against mine. "I promise to help defeat the shadow fae king in exchange for your sacrifice."

"I promise I'll give you your sacrifice if you help me defeat the fae king."

A shock raced up my arm, down my body. The magic coursed through my body then settled on my left shoulder. I pulled the neck of my shirt down and looked at it. The symbol of the Bonecrown witches was inked in my skin, like a temporary tattoo.

Corvina showed me her shoulder, the same symbol in her own skin. The wicked smile on her lips stretched wider. "It's done." She waved her hand at me, as if I was a bug she didn't want to bother with. "Myra, take her back to the manor. I'll come see you later."

"Yes, my queen," Myra said.

I turned to follow Myra, but another before we could leave the garden, another witch showed up.

She bowed her head to the queen. "We have company."

I FROZE AT THE CASTLE'S ENTRANCE, STARING AT THE newcomers at the bottom of the stairs—Daleigh, Ariella, Kayden, and Wyatt. I hadn't been naive to think they wouldn't try to find me, I just didn't think they would find me this fast.

"What are you doing here?" I asked them in a croak. I stood in between Corvina and Myra, with a dozen witches behind us, ready to attack in case they demonstrate ill-intentions toward their queen.

"What are *you* doing here?" Daleigh asked, taking a step forward. The witches behind me tensed, and Daleigh stopped. "Weren't you running away from them?"

"My oh my," Corvina started, her voice gaining a fake honeyed tone. "You haven't told them your plans." She glanced at me, a mischievous glint in her dark eyes. She lifted her hand, showing the fresh cut on her palm. "Farrah and I enacted a blood pact."

"W-what?" Ariella asked, her eyes huge.

Meanwhile, I looked everywhere but at Wyatt, who stood right in the middle of the group, his body rigid, the frustration and disappointment rolling off him in waves. If I look at him, if I met his gaze, my determination might waver. And now I had the blood pact to answer to. There was no coming back.

"It's done," I told them.

"What did you promise her?" Daleigh asked, his voice faint.

Corvina was the one to answer it. "My witches and I will help you defeat the fae king. In return, Farrah will serve as my sacrifice, as she had always been intended for."

"No," Daleigh whispered.

I inhaled deeply. I couldn't be swayed by him. By Wyatt. By anyone. "You better go now," I said, my tone short. Flat.

"Farrah, can I speak with you."

That was Wyatt. I stilled and dared glancing his way. "We have nothing to talk about."

His fists clenched and unclenched, and his jaw worked hard. "Drollmor might cause us trouble while we're figuring out a way to defeat the fae king, so we're planning on going after him." He shifted his weight. "We were wondering, *I* was wondering, if you wouldn't like to come with us. To help us."

I felt Corvina's eagerness beside me. She was loving the awkwardness and tension of the scene before her.

Finally, the witch queen spoke. "I wouldn't mind if you went. We can work on the terms of the blood pact after." She glanced at the others. "You're invited to stay until Farrah comes to a decision." She gestured to Myra. "Please, escort them to the manor and make them comfortable."

"Yes, my queen." Myra bowed her head to Corvina, then faced the group. "Follow me."

Reluctantly, Daleigh, Ariella, and Kayden followed Myra through the castle. Wyatt hesitated, but finally walked by me and went with the others.

"I'm going for a walk," I whispered to Corvina, before dashing down the steps and disappearing in the garden beside the castle.

I needed time to think, to clear my mind, to reassess my purpose, my intentions, my duty. I couldn't stay close to Wyatt and let him crumble my resolve with just one glance.

It was harder than it should have been.

4

Myra told us this was the same manor Luana and Keeran had stayed before, and now was Farrah's. And Rusty's. The fucking cat was curled at the top of the stairs, as if he owned the place.

"Where did you come from?" I asked him, but as a cat, he just meowed and went back to napping.

While Daleigh, Ariella, and Kayden explored the manor, I sent a message to Rey and Erin. I hadn't talked to them in many years, but I knew that if I was able to reach the Blackthorn Hunters Academy, I could reach them. In the message, I told them I needed help with a higher demon. Hopefully, it would be a quick thing and they wouldn't be too busy to come lend a hand.

After, I explored the manor, hoping Farrah would come in at any time and I would be able to talk to her.

But she didn't come. Not even to sleep. I knew because I barely slept all fucking night. Each creak in the wood flooring, or the sound of the breeze pushing on the windows woke me up and sent my heart in overdrive. But it was never Farrah. Her scent was fading from the manor, since she hadn't been in here for many, many hours.

In the morning, I had breakfast with the others. They seemed eager to go and deal with Drollmor, but I told them I was waiting for answers, not only from Farrah, but from two demon hunter friends.

After that, I went for a walk on the manor's garden, but my mind was in the fucking blood pact Farrah had just struck. Why the fuck had she done that? What the fuck had she been thinking?

If she was here, I would be yelling at her, for sure, but she was avoiding me, I knew that.

So I did the next best thing I could think of. I went to see Corvina.

As I expected, I was seen coming toward the palace, and two witches escorted me to the throne room, where Corvina was, seated on her black bone throne, looking very intimidating and evil.

I halted several feet from her and swallowed hard. I wasn't afraid of her, but she definitely could strike me down with one fucking snap of her fingers. Besides, Farrah's life was now in her hands.

"My oh my," she said, a smile spreading over her lips. "I knew you would come to see me."

"Why is that?"

"Because you're Farrah's mate. I knew you would come intercede on her behalf."

"Will it work?"

She shook her head once. "The deal is sealed. There's nothing you can do to null it."

"What if I take her place?" I asked, knowing it was a hard call. The Bonecrown witches had been after Farrah for many years now. They wouldn't let another one take her place. If it was that easy, it would have already been done.

Slowly, Corvina rose from her throne and stalked to me, her dark eyes one mine. I didn't dare breaking her stare, lest she thought I was weak. "The thing is, dear Wyatt, Farrah is powerful. She always has been. And now with the frost pendant, she's even more. Her sacrifice will be delicious." She walked in a circle around me, watching me. I stared at the wall straight ahead. "You're a powerful werewolf, but not like her. Unless you could suddenly become stronger, I can't make a deal with you."

My jaw clenched and my insides tightened. I was a normal werewolf, with normal werewolf strength, normal werewolf agility. There was nothing special about me.

"What if I could change that?"

She halted before me. "If somehow you become more powerful than Farrah, then I'll consider your proposition." She whirled around and went back to her throne. "Now go. I have other matters to attend to."

I wanted to argue, to ask her if she knew of any spells I could use to help me become more powerful, but I didn't want to push my luck. With my tail in between my legs, I dragged my feet out of the throne room.

In need of some fresh air, I stepped out of the castle. I didn't see them, but I felt the witches following me, making sure I didn't stir trouble. They didn't need to worry about me. Other than the pent up frustration and my wolf begging me to go for a run that would deplete my energy, so I could finally relax, I didn't plan on doing anything.

Not right now at least.

I let my feet take me, until I was in the middle of a green and luscious garden, staring at the stone bench in the middle of a well-manicured clearing—where Farrah was seated.

She had her eyes closed, her face tilted up, as if enjoying the warmth of the sun shining down on her. A pang cut through my heart. She was so fucking beautiful and all I wanted to do was go to her, hold her against me, and never letting go.

"I don't see you, but I can feel you," she said, her voice soft. She lowered her chin and opened her eyes, staring at me with those brilliant blue eyes. "Were you following me?"

I shook my head. "I can honestly say I wasn't. I was just walking around, clear—"

"Clearing your head," she said, nodding. "I understand that."

She fell quiet and averted her eyes. Fuck, I couldn't just pretend this was all right. That she wasn't my mate and she hadn't just signed a death warrant.

In four long strides, I reached her and sat beside her on the bench. "Talk to me."

She scooted away from me, as far as the bench allowed her to go. "There's nothing to talk about."

"Farrah, we're mates and—"

"Yes, we are mates, but being mates doesn't mean we'll live happily ever after. My life has been on the line since I was born, Wyatt. I knew I was destined to die young ... I just didn't think I would find my mate before that. Don't you see? Loving you just complicates things."

I winced with the power of her words. Though, I knew what she meant. She had been promised to the Bonecrown witches, then to Prince Lark, and despite all that, there was still the curse which dictated she would lose her powers and die like a human if she ever loved and stayed with a non-fae. Either way, she was heading toward death.

It wasn't fucking fair.

"There has to be a way out of this." I gestured to us, to the place around us. "Out of all of this. I have to believe that."

She shook her head. "Sometimes, bad things happen to good people. That's life."

"Farrah, I—"

"Excuse me," a voice said. Farrah and I turned to see a witch standing at the edge of the garden. "Two demon hunters arrived."

I STARED AT WYATT. "DEMON HUNTERS?"

One corner of his lips tugged up. "I called some friends to help us out." He walked away, following the witch to the front of the castle, and I followed him.

Rey and Erin walked up the path toward the castle's entrance, flanked by a dozen witches, but they didn't seem fazed by it. And, when their eyes landed on Wyatt, both of them smiled. Wyatt grabbed Rey's arm in a thigh grip and then he hugged Erin.

"I was told you two have already met Farrah," Wyatt said, gesturing to me.

I raised my hand and waved at them. "Hello again."

Erin's smile widened and Rey nodded at me. The first and only time I had seen them before was when I was trying to escape General Auron and some shadow fae who were intent on bringing me to Prince Lark by force. They helped get away from them, and from the demon hunters who thought I was the one causing trouble. Back then, the two of them had looked striking, but not like this. Looking older and wiser, Erin and Rey donned black leather uniforms, their eyes shining in contrast to one another—Erin's were bright gold, and Rey's were a silvery gray.

They formed a beautiful couple.

"So," Rey started, looking at Wyatt. "What the fuck did you do this time?"

"Hm." Wyatt ran a hand over his hair. "Why don't we go back to the manor and talk? It's almost lunchtime anyway."

Rey narrowed his eyes at Wyatt, but just dipped his chin in agreement.

We started moving toward the manor, and for a moment, I thought the witches would trust us, but of course I was wrong. They gave us some space but followed us as we took our friends to the manor.

At the manor, Wyatt led them inside, then turned to the witches. "Hm, can you inform Myra we have guests? And to send lunch? Thanks."

Shocked, they stared at one another.

And I almost laughed at Wyatt's boldness.

That would probably have been the first time I had laughed in ... I didn't even know how long.

Ariella, Kayden, and Daleigh joined us for lunch at the large dining room in the manor. We only exchanged small talk while we ate, because I didn't want to spoil their appetite. Knowing Rey, he would have a fit when I told them what I had done.

To my surprise, he didn't. Neither did Erin. They just looked at each other, a loving and trusting gaze. They might not agree with my methods, but they would have gone to the same lengths for each other. That was crystal clear.

"How do we find this demon?" Ariella asked, her voice quiet. She was still mad at me, and I guessed she would always be, but I knew she was eager to find some demons and kick their asses.

"Because of the soul selling deal, Wyatt probably has a direct connection to Drollmor," Erin explained. "We can cast a quick, but painful spell to track him."

Farrah sucked in a sharp breath. "Painful?"

Rey nodded, shifting his gaze to me. "Are you up for that?"

"You know I am," was all I said.

I could feel Farrah's eyes on me as we moved from the dining room to the living room, her worry palpable in the air. Like a well-oiled machine, Erin and Rey pushed the tables and armchairs back, creating a large space in the middle of the room, and stood in front of one another, waiting for me.

"Come," Erin said, beckoning me forward.

I walked up to them. "What do I do?"

"Just stand there." Rey extended his arm and the Shadowblade appeared in his hand—the sword of the demon hunters. I gaped at it when he brought it up toward me. "Relax, I just need a drop of blood."

Somewhere behind me, Farrah let out an exhale. "Blood. Everything, every damn spell needs blood."

I frowned. Was she talking about the fucking blood pact she had done with Queen Corvina? Then that was on her.

Rey pressed the sharp side of the blade against the tip of my finger, drawing blood. He lowered his arm, the sword disappearing, then closed his hand over my finger. He closed his eyes for a second, and when he opened them, they were completely black.

His half-demon side showing.

The magic rushed from him to me, coursing through my body, first itching like a nasty scratch, then burning, like boiling water. I groaned, trying to brace myself, but the pain was too much. I fell on my knees.

"Don't," I heard Erin saying. "Stay back. He'll be fine."

I sucked in shallow gasps, trying to control the pain, to control myself. Soon, the magic left me again, but the pain remained.

Rey let go of my hand and I fell forward, slapping the floor with my hands.

"I know where he is," he said, his eyes returning to normal.

Breathing hard, my muscles screaming, I pushed up. "Let's go."

"You can't go like this," Farrah said, showing up beside me. She grabbed my arm, as if she could keep me steady.

"She's right," Erin said. "You're too weak and the pain is probably still making its way through you." She glanced at Rey past my shoulder and nodded. Her eyes returned to me. "Rest now. We'll leave tomorrow morning."

I opened my mouth to protest, but Farrah tugged my arm. "Just ... stay quiet and come with me."

7

From the moment Erin and Rey said they needed to do a spell in order to find Drollmor, my insides twisted. I knew it meant using Wyatt somehow. Though I was glad they only needed a drop of blood, it still made me sick to see him in so much pain.

Ariella helped me carry him up the stairs and deposited him in the bed of the room he had taken as his yesterday.

"If you need anything, just call," Ariella said, retreating from the room.

"Thank you," I whispered, before returning my attention to Wyatt. Groaning, he pressed his hand on his middle and curled into himself. Helpless, I sat beside him on the bed. "Where does it hurt?"

"Everywhere," he rasped.

I glanced over him, trying to find any wounds other than the little prick in his fingertip, but I couldn't find anything.

"I wish I could help you," I said, my voice faint. I lay my hands on his side and thigh, wishing I could do something. Use some magic to transfer the pain to me, to extinguish.

Then it happened.

My hands warmed and power filled my veins. But it wasn't my usual frost related power. It was something else.

Wyatt's eyes widened and he fixed them on me. "W-what's going on?" His voice trembled, and his body shuddered as the power traveled from me to him.

Slowly, his shaking lessened, he uncurled his long body, and even the little prick in his finger disappeared.

Wyatt sat up. "It's gone. The pain, the prick. It's all gone." He reached over and took my hands in his. "What did you do?"

I shrugged, as perplexed as he was. "I don't know." I glanced at our joined hands, trying to understand. "I mean, I heard of fae who could heal, but I had never met one." Probably because all of them still lived in the fae realm. Still, that was a legend I had eagerly listened to as a child, as if it was another fairy tale. "Perhaps this wasn't healing."

Disentangling one of his hands from mine, Wyatt showed me his finger. "Yes, it was." He tugged me closer to him, and stunned, I didn't resist. "You're amazing, Farrah."

I stilled. "Wyatt ..."

"What? What excuse are you going to tell me now so you can run from me? I know you love me as much as I love you. I don't understand why you can't just *be* with me."

"Because!" I gritted my teeth. I tried pulling my hands

from his, but he only held tighter, without hurting me. "You know why. If I stay with you, I'll die anyway."

"But I'll die too."

"Yeah, but you're a werewolf. You'll live a lot longer than a human. I'll die and leave you alone for more than half of your life. So why get more attached, why love each other more, just to suffer in the end?"

He shook his head. "You can't think like that. Even if I had immortality like you, it's not guaranteed I wouldn't die of something else. But you do it anyway. You get involved, you love, because the moments, the memories ... they are worth it. If you die before me, I'll have at least the memories of all the time we had together." He leaned over me. "And I want that, Farrah. I want every fucking second you can give me."

His body irradiated power and strength and warmth and everything I wanted and shouldn't have. But when he lowered his head to mine, I couldn't fight it. I couldn't say no to him, not again. Not ever.

With a long sigh, I melted.

Wyatt pressed his mouth on mine and I parted my lips to him, letting him in, letting him take all of me.

I wrapped my arms around him. "I'm yours," I whispered against his lips. "Always was, always will be."

He claimed my mouth with his, deepening the kiss and lying us back in the bed.

In no time, our clothes were gone and our bodies were joined as one.

I DID LEAVE WYATT ALONE IN BED AGAIN, BUT THIS TIME I had every intention of coming back. It was just ... when I woke up in the middle of the night, tangled in his arms and legs, with my side buried on his chest, his heartbeat steady and strong against me, a panic started deep in my core.

How could I do this? How could I just close my eyes and pretend everything was okay? That soon Corvina and her witches wouldn't kill me?

But as his warmth seeped into me, his breathing washing over the skin on my neck and giving me delicious goosebumps, I realized that it didn't matter. This was where I was supposed to be. With my mate, even if only for a month.

A week.

Or a day.

Emotion filled my chest and tears threatened to spill. Before I could wake him up, I slipped from the bed, wrapped myself with a robe, tied it around my middle, and walked out the bedroom. I needed a little bit of fresh air, then I would be all right.

I stepped out of the manor through the back, halted at the edge of the stone porch, and inhaled deeply, welcoming the crisp air of the dark night.

"Can't sleep?"

I jumped, already reaching for my powers, but my brain worked, and I recognized the voice even before turning to see him. "What are you doing here, Daleigh?"

My brother slouched on the stone floor, his eyes to the stars dotting the night sky beyond. He shrugged. "I woke up and couldn't go back to sleep. Thought some fresh air would do me some good."

I knew exactly what he meant. I sat down at the edge of the porch, a couple of feet from him. "I healed Wyatt earlier."

He sat straight. "What? How?"

"I don't know. I just did it. Like those legends we always heard about when kids."

"Legend?" He scoffed. "They weren't legends, Farrah. There are fae who can heal, it's just very, very rare, most stories about them were embellished and became legends."

"How ... how didn't I know?"

"Probably because you were young when we were banished, and we didn't have any healing fae with us. We stopped talking about many things from the fae realm, because it hurt too much. That must have been one of those things."

"It makes sense," I whispered, trying to come to terms that what I had done was real and not unknown. I only wished I could find out more about it.

I looked up and glanced at the stars. Here in the middle of the mountains, darkness was almost absolute, and the stars shone bright, like a dot-covered blanket in the night sky.

"I'm sorry."

I whipped my head back to my brother. "What?"

"I'm sorry," he said again, a little louder. "For all I put you through. I know just saying sorry will never cut it, but it's all I can say or do right now." He let out a long sigh.

"When you got chosen to be sent to the Bonecrown witches, I should have done something. I don't know, maybe hid you away, or even sent someone else, as cruel as it sounds." He paused. "And when you made your promise to Prince Lark and he offered me a bonus, I should have denied it. I should have helped you hide from him, not hunt you down to hand you to him."

"I was really mad at you for all of that, but I also understood why you did it." And that was the truth. "I was your sister, but I was also one life against hundreds. Your choices reflected that of a good leader."

He scoffed. "A good leader who got his people imprisoned and tortured by the shadow fae."

"You couldn't have known Lark would lie."

"I should have known," he said. "Everyone knows his father was pure evil, and the apple never lands too far from the tree."

I scooted closer to him and placed a hand over his arm. "Despite everything, I forgive you."

"I don't deserve your forgiveness."

"That's for me to decide. But since I do forgive you, I think now you should try to forgive yourself."

He scoffed again. "Very unlikely."

I patted his arm. "I have faith in you."

"That makes one of us." He glanced down at his arms for a second before looking at me again. "Will you still forgive me if I kidnap you and try to hide you from the witches this time."

An amused, but sad smile graced my lips. "Don't even try."

"If I don't try, then I won't have changed, will I?"

"Daleigh, I'm warning you." I wiped the smile from my face and stared at him as serious as I could. "This is my choice this time. Please, don't ruin it."

He held my gaze, his blue eyes shining with defiance. But finally, he nodded. "I'll try."

8

I half-expected Farrah to be gone when I woke up, but to my surprise, she was curled beside me. A smile spread over my lips and I reached for her, scooting closer to her, pressing my body to her.

She grumbled and I laughed, way too fucking happy about this.

"Good morning," I whispered, nestling my face in her neck. She grumbled again, but stretched her head back, giving me more access to her neck. I grazed my teeth on her skin and she inhaled sharply.

"Morning," she rasped. She wound her arms around my shoulders and pulled me closer.

"This is a nice surprise."

"What is?"

I pulled back, so I could look at her. "Having you in my bed in the morning."

Her eyes darkened. "Wyatt—"

"No, it's okay. I would rather not remember the other

times." I ran my hand around her jaw, down her neck. "Just this one." I traveled my fingertips over her collarbone and dipped them down in between her breasts.

Farrah's back arched with my touch. "Keep that up and I won't ever leave this bed."

I suppressed a chuckle. "Promise?" I leaned into her, pressing a soft kiss on her lips. "Unfortunately, we gotta go. The others are waiting for us."

Farrah locked her arms and legs around me. "They can wait."

A slow smile took over my lips as I pressed my body against her, grounding my hips on her, ripping a moan from her throat. "That they can do."

IN THE END, DROLLMOR WASN'T FAR FROM WHERE WE WERE. After our last encounter and my escape, he was probably tracking me down in order to collect his dues. We filled three cars: Queen Corvina, Mira, two other witches, and Farrah in one, since Corvina wanted Farrah close to her; Daleigh, Kayden, Ariella, and Erin in a second one, which left Rey and me on the last one, which was exactly how I wanted.

The sun was just starting to show up behind the mountain when Rey took the wheel and drove out, leading the way to where Drollmor was staying, the other cars following behind.

Two minutes in the road, he smacked his lips. "So, when will you tell me why the fuck you pushed the girls to the other cars and had us alone?" He glanced at me before staring back at the road. "And don't even try to deny it. I know you."

I should have known I couldn't fool him. "Well, I wanted to ask you something." I paused, unsure if after my question, he would stop the car and just punch me. "Is there a way to obtain power from a demon? I don't know what kind of power? Magic, strength, whatever. Do you know anything about it?"

Rey pressed his lips together. "What exactly are you looking for?"

"Just a way to get stronger, more powerful."

"There might be a way to absorb a demon's power, but it'll eventually kill you."

"It's okay, I figured that."

"And why would you need more power?"

I decided to start from the beginning. "It's just ... Farrah made a deal with the Bonecrown Witch Queen. If Corvina helps us kill the fae king, Farrah will willingly sacrifice herself for the witches, whatever ridiculous ritual they do to increase their powers. I went to Corvina and offered myself instead. She said she wouldn't accept it unless I was stronger than Farrah, or just as strong." I sighed. "My intention is to gain enough power to be the sacrifice in Farrah's place, so I'll die in the end anyway." Saying it out loud was stranger than I first thought. Scarier. But it didn't matter. I wouldn't back up from this idea even if I had to ask Rey to fucking tie me down in order to keep my fear contained.

Rey opened his mouth, then closed it again. His hands

tightened around the wheel. "I'm so close to yelling at you and try to convince you that you're making a bad choice, but the truth is ... I would do the same thing for Erin. I would gladly lay down my life if it meant she could live."

"So, you're going to tell me what I have to do?"

Rey nodded.

And then he told me what I had to do.

I TURNED THE CORNER AND ENTERED THE ALLEY. JUST LIKE Rey said, there was a large metal door at the end. I knocked it on it. A second later, a man opened, his wide shoulders filling the doorframe.

"What do you want?" he barked with his deep voice.

"I'm here to talk to Drollmor," I said. "Tell him Wyatt is waiting for him at the alley."

The man cocked an eyebrow at me, but didn't question it. He closed the door again.

He could just ignore me and not pass the message to Drollmor, but for some reason, I knew he would. I backed away from the door, halting right in the middle of the alley, and waited.

Rey and Erin told me there was a pub hidden behind the door where neutral and higher demons like to hang out. If I entered the pub, I was done for. It would be hard to help me out in there, much less get out.

So I decided to bait Drollmor into coming to me. Since he had been after me for a while now, I knew he wouldn't say no.

A couple of minutes later, the door opened and Drollmor stepped out the door, followed by a handful of his lackeys—all lesser demons. I didn't know if Drollmor thought I was just stupid for coming here alone, or if he knew I had friends surrounding the alley, ready for a fight. I didn't care either. As long as we took care of him and this damn contract for my soul was ripped apart, it was all fair play.

"When Johnny told me a Wyatt was out here calling for me, I thought he was mistaken," Drollmor said, his eyes running over me, as if sizing up his prize. He still wore the same skin as the last time I saw him: olive skin and he wore an olive skin and short, brown hair, with the sides neatly shaved. His face was angular and his body was big, as if he was a heavy weightlifter. "But here you are. What do I owe this pleasure?" His brow furrowed. "You aren't here to ask for an extension of our contract, right? 'Cause you know I can't do that." He tilted his head. "But I doubt you're here just to hand yourself over. Then why are you here, boy?"

"To give you a chance," I said. I knew Drollmor would never back out of the deal. And even if he did, I needed to kill him if I wanted to steal his power. I needed to do more than that.

Drollmor cackled. "A chance? To what? Call out our deal? Never."

"Then I guess I'll need to kill you."

The amusement left the higher demon's face. "I grow tired of your games, boy." He bared his elongating teeth. "I will kill you and I'll take your soul with me."

He threw his hands out, his dark powers coming at me.

But I was ready for him.

I rolled out of the way.

His lesser demons ran to me.

And my friends emerged from the shadows.

A battle began all around Drollmor and me. I quickly took off my shirt and shifted into my werewolf, not caring that my pants ripped into shreds.

I let Drollmor think he would face only me for a few seconds, then Rey and Erin turned to us. I wasn't here to play fair, I was here to win.

Rey's and Erin's Shadowblade appeared in their hands, and they advanced toward Drollmor, their movements mirrored, as if they had rehearsed this before.

Maybe they had, having fought side by side many times before.

Drollmor's attention split between the three of us, but he couldn't take us all at the same time. When we attacked, it didn't take him five seconds to make a mistake and fall.

Eri ran her Shadowblade across his back, and Rey had sliced his front thighs. The demon folded over on the hard ground, a howl of pain exploding from his throat.

I jumped on him, closed my jaws around his neck, and killed him.

Erin immediately turned back to the lesser demons—more had come from inside the pub and were fighting our friends.

Rey paused. He gave me a quick nod, then joined Erin.

It was only me and Drollmor's body now.

A sudden sickness curled in my stomach, but I pushed past it. I held my breath and did what Rey told me: I opened up Drollmor's neck, found his jugular, and drank his blood.

His still warm blood.

The moment I swallowed the last ounce, pain like no one assaulted me, making me yelp and curl on the ground. Bile rose to my throat and I thought I would throw the blood back up.

But after an intense jolt of pain, it was all gone.

The pain, the nausea.

In its place, a humming began inside me, like energy building up.

Drollmor's powers.

I joined the others and in no time, we cleared out the alley. No other demon came from the pub. While everyone pretended to be busy cleaning up, I shifted back into my human form, Rey handed me some pants he had taken off from a body, and I dressed myself again.

"It's done," I said, my eyes on Drollmor's body. I had rolled him around, so his back was up, and no one could see the huge hole in his neck. I didn't want to answer the questions that might bring forth.

"You're free now?" Farrah asked, her voice low. If only she knew what I had done, and why I had done it.

I nodded.

"Good," Corvina snapped. "Now can we go? We have much to do if we're going to defeat the fae king." Her eyes lingered on Farrah. I could hear her unspoken words: *and if I'm going to have you as my sacrifice.*

Thankfully, she didn't say that out loud.

"Let's go," I said, turning away from the alley. My eyes

landed on Ariella, who was leaned on a sticky, dirty wall, her skin paler than usual. "Ariella, what is it?"

"I'm ..." She pulled her hand from her stomach, her fingers coming out red.

"It's blood," Kayden said, her voice urgent. "She's hurt!"

"No, I'm ..." Ariella didn't finish her sentence. Instead, she collapsed to the ground.

9

I weaved past the others and knelt beside Ariella. I didn't really know what I was doing, just that I had to try it. I placed my hands on the ugly, deep slash across her stomach, pressing against the oozing blood, and called on my magic.

My mind was scattered and my hands shook, unable to focus. Before, I had healed Wyatt without meaning to. His life hadn't been at risk. This was different. Ariella was bleeding out right before my eyes. I had to find a way to focus and do this, however it was done.

"I can't," I said, my voice breaking. "It's not working."

"We have to take her to a hospital," Rey said. "Or somewhere else for supernaturals."

"This is nasty," Erin said, her tone grim. "She'll need more than a healer."

"I know a place we can take her." Kayden knelt beside me. "I know of a highly powerful healer place back in the fae realm."

I stared at her. "You do?"

She shrugged. "At least, I hope they are still open. Who knows? With the shadow fae king, they might have closed it."

"We're wasting time," I urged. "Let's just go."

Daleigh picked up Ariella in his arms, and Kayden pulled her medallion out and opened the portal.

"Hm." Rey ran a hand over his hair. "I think Erin and I are done here." He glanced at Ariella, his eyes dull. "I don't think we can help with that."

"It's fine," Wyatt said, turning to them. "Thank you for all your help."

Rey grabbed Wyatt's arm, his grip tight. "Good luck, man."

Wyatt nodded. "Thanks."

As he turned to say goodbye to Erin, Corvina stepped on my way.

"Where do you think you're going, dear?" She placed her hands on her waist.

"To the fae realm," I answered.

"They don't need you there either."

She was right, but I couldn't just stay here and wait for news. "She's my friend ..."

I thought I would have to argue more, to come up with a good, sensible explanation, but Corvina just sighed. "Myra, take the others and go back. I'll go with Farrah." She leaned closer to me, giving me her most wicked smile. "To make sure you won't run away."

Kayden tsked. "Can you all stop whatever you're doing?

If we want to save Ariella, we have to go. Now!" She pointed to the portal.

Daleigh was already on the other side, Ariella fainted on his arms. Wyatt went up next. Then Corvina and I. Kayden was last.

Once we were on the other side, I looked past the portal once more. Rey and Erin waved at us.

Then the portal closed and they were gone.

KAYDEN HAD OPENED THE PORTAL RIGHT IN FRONT OF A large palace made of light gray stones, hidden in what seemed the forest that covered the border between the Blaze and the Wind fae.

As we approached the grand stairs at the castle's entrance, the giant doors opened, and fae dressed in white rushed out—fae of all kinds: blaze, frost, wind ... but no shadow fae.

"What happened?" a female frost fae asked, gesturing for Daleigh to come in.

"A demon attack," he said, following her inside. "She already bled a whole lot."

"We'll do what we can," a male blaze fae told us.

A female blaze fae turned to us. "Stay here at the foyer while we work on her. Someone will come to help you."

They disappeared under a large archway, where other fae walked by, all wearing white. Some had other fae under their arms, all of them wearing what looked like hospital gowns. Their patients.

"This place is incredible," I heard Daleigh say from beside me.

I followed his gaze and looked around, taking in this strange castle. The foyer looked one out of the frost court, except for all the pillars and archways made of stones, and the wood accents here and there. I also saw some details that reminded me of the blaze fae. This palace seemed to be a mix of all the courts, which only made more curious about it.

"Ah, there you are," a voice said.

We turned to it.

I gaped.

"Spencer?" Wyatt said from my side.

I stared at my mate. "You know him?"

"Yes." Wyatt glanced at me. "He was the one who gave me that blue pendant I gave to you. He said you need it."

I slipped my hand in my pocket and held the frost pendant neatly tucked in there. I really had needed it. Without it, I wouldn't have been able to kill Prince Lark or escape the Shade Fortress.

"How ... how did you know?" I asked Spencer.

The old fae shrugged. "Wisdom comes with age." He threw a white towel at Daleigh, who was covered in Ariella's blood.

"Thanks," Daleigh said, wiping some of the blood away.

Spencer frowned and looked around me. "Where's my cat?"

I stilled. Shit. "Hm, back in the Bonecrown coven. He's fine."

"I know he is," he muttered, though he didn't look convinced.

"Wait." It was Wyatt's turn to stare at me. "You've met Spencer too?"

I nodded. "Yes. He asked me to take care of his cat. In return, he gave me something I wanted." My voice lowered, because I didn't want to say it was an ingredient for poison. That would make me sound like a ruthless murderer and I certainly wasn't that.

"Wait," Daleigh started. "What's going on here?"

I explained to him that Wyatt and I had briefly met Spencer before on separate occasions, but both of us had no idea who he was or what he did.

"So, hm," Wyatt tried again. "You're a healer?"

"Something like that," Spencer said. "I'm the owner of this castle and leader of the healer fae."

Kayden pointed to the stairs, where two fae walked by. "You must have plenty of fae here. Why haven't you fought against the fae king?"

"As healers, we're pacifist," Spencer explained. "We won't fight in any wars, but we'll heal everyone who needs it." A small smile spread over his lips. "Speaking of that, I have news that your angel friend will be all right. She just needs to rest for a few days." He glanced at all of us, one by one. His eyes lingered a little too long on Corvina, but if he was worried about her, he didn't show. "You're welcome to stay here until she can leave."

Spencer looked at us expectantly, as if waiting for an answer.

Daleigh, Kayden, Corvina, Wyatt, and I exchanged glances. They all nodded, even if Corvina didn't look too happy about it.

I turned to Spencer. "We'll stay."

Even though it was late at night, Spencer had some of the other healers show us around the castle. We had a quick tour of the main castle side, the common area, the hospital wing, the gardens, etc. We were taken first to the long dining room, which looked like a cafeteria with long, wooden tables, and a bar to one side where the food was served. We ate in silence—everyone was taking in the place on their own—and then we were escorted to our bedrooms at the guests' wing.

Accordingly Ares, the blaze fae who served as our guide, we could go anywhere freely, but the hospital wing. Since it was full of sick and hurt fae and other supernaturals, we had to be allowed in there by Spencer, and escorted into a visitor area. We promised not to go there, unless we were called to see Ariella, who was doing well, as we were told.

The guests' wing was made up of several simple suites, and Farrah and I had been placed in one of them.

Tired after a long day or fighting and running and exploring, we barely exchanged any words while we took a quick bath and cuddled in bed. In minutes, Farrah was asleep in my arms.

I waited a couple of hours, to make sure everyone else was sleeping too, and slipped from the bed.

The guests' wing was eerily quiet and unguarded as I walked through it, and out into the dark night.

A chilling breeze met me, making me shiver. Fucking temperamental weather. Being on the border of Wind and Frost Courts, this place seemed to get cold first thing in the morning, then it suddenly became too hot, and later it was cold again. For a werewolf like me who liked the warm weather, this was almost as much torture as standing in the Frost Court all day long.

Despite that, it was a beautiful night, and millions of stars blanketed the dark sky.

I walked away from the castle, my ears straining for any sound and my nose placing each scent. But there was no one around. No other fae, except for the ones inside the castle, no guards.

How could these people just stay here like sitting ducks when the shadow fae king could come and destroy them at any minute?

I didn't bother thinking about that. Instead, I stopped a few feet into the forest, in a small opening among several tall, thick trees. Since drinking Drollmor's blood, I felt his powers spreading through me, filling me, becoming mine. I couldn't wait to test them.

But how did I start?

I spread my hands wide and closed my eyes, trying to feel the power inside me. Was this how Farrah worked her frost magic? By just thinking about it and ordering around?

This felt fucking stupid.

But what other choice I had? I closed my eyes and focused on the sensation inside of me. This strain of power, this worm that buried itself in my veins, that hitched a hike with my blood ...

And I told it to do *something*.

The air around me hummed and I opened my eyes just in time to see as black flames appeared over my outstretched hands. My jaw hit the floor. I moved my arms side to side, and the flames following, taking shape after my movement. I flexed my fingers, making a claw, and the flames curled into black balls.

This was fucking awesome.

The thrumming inside me increased and I just knew there was more.

So I let it go and allowed the power to take over me. Going with these instincts, I shifted.

But instead of turning into my usual light brown wolf, I turned into a fucking big demon-wolf. I had heard about these before, but I had never seen one.

And now I was one!

Pure powers rambled inside me as I pounced around, testing my new shape. This wolf was a lot larger than my normal one, almost twice its size. It was stronger, faster, and could jump further. My vision and hearing, which were already great, were now out of this world. I could hear everything for miles, and I could see in the dark as if it was plain day.

I bit down on a thick fallen trunk, and my new long, sharp teeth snapped it in half as if it was a toothpick.

And just as awesome: my clothes hadn't ripped off when I shifted back!

This was fucking badass.

I froze as a distance sound reached my ears. Farrah had woken up and was looking for me. I didn't know exactly what she was doing, but she called me a couple of times, then padded her way out of the guests' wing.

First, she went to the wrong side, to the front of the castle.

Then she turned to the back.

Still in wolf form, I went to meet her.

She was wandering the back garden, a thin blanket wrapped over her the thin nightgown she was wearing, looking side to side, when I stepped out of the forest.

Sucking a sharp inhale, she stopped and looked at me. She let go of the blanket, raising her hands to call her magic.

I quickly shifted in front of her, my clothes intact. "It's me!"

She gaped at me. "What ... How ... ?"

I walked to her, almost skipping in such excitement. "I asked Rey for help to steal some of Drollmor's powers before killing him," I told her, leaving out crucial parts of the story. Like the fact I had drunk his blood like a fucking vampire and stolen *all* of his powers. "I thought it would be a good idea since we'll face the fae king next."

She stared at me for a moment, a slow smiling spreading over her lips. "That's incredible." She grasped my arms. "But you're okay, right? No side effects?"

I shook my head. "Nope." Just that I would die for it sometime soon, but she didn't need to know about that. Not yet. I slipped my hand on hers. "How about we take a stroll through the garden?"

She narrowed her eyes at me. "At this time of night?"

I shrugged. "Why not?"

She nodded and I tugged her close. We began walking slowly across the garden, but we weren't looking at the bushes or flowers or benches. We were looking up. At the moon and the stars.

"I like this," she said, gluing her side to mine and holding my entire arm in front of her.

"Me too," I whispered. I leaned into her and placed a quick kiss on the top of her head. We entered a part of the garden surrounded by tall hedges and with a wooden bench on the side. I suddenly stopped and faced her. "Farrah, I just need to say something." She blinked at me, serious. "I know that our time is limited," because I would die in her place, "but my love for you isn't. It won't ever be. I will always love you. Forever. No matter what. Remember that."

Her eyebrows curled down and she looked at our joined hands. The next second, she wrapped her arms around my back and pulled me to her. "I love you too, you idiot."

She pressed her lips on mine, and I lost it.

I slid my hands around her waist and pulled her to me,

pressing her body to mine. I leaned into her, deepening the kiss as much as it was possible. I wanted to taste her, I wanted to savor her, I wanted to imprint this to my mind, until I was gone.

"If you keep this going, I'll take you right here," I whispered against her lips.

She pulled back just an inch and cocked one eyebrow at me. She pushed me back, until my legs hit the wooden bench and I fell seated on it. Then she crawled over me, straddling me.

"Who says that's not what I want?" she asked, her voice husky.

Holy fuck. If I wasn't a goner before, I was now. In an instant, I was hard and ready for her. Feeling that, she pressed her lips on mine, while quickly pulling her night-gown up her legs and pushing the waist of my pants down, and in one single movement, she sat over me again, taking me inside of her.

I let out a sigh of relief and pleasure.

We belonged together. That was fucking certain.

Right there, in the middle of the garden in the healer's refugee, Farrah rode me, taking us both to new heights. So high, I wasn't sure I wanted to ever come fucking down.

11

DESPITE SLEEPING ONLY A LITTLE LAST NIGHT—ALL WYATT'S fault for tempting me with his perfect mouth and body—I woke up early. Wyatt had seen me sneaking out of the bed and held on to me.

"It's not even eight in the morning yet," he grumbled against my neck.

I laughed, but was able to extricate myself from him. He grumbled some more, turned to the side, and went back to snoring. I smiled at his beautiful sleeping form, got dressed in sensible clothes, and went to find some breakfast.

The real reason I had woken up early, though, was because I wanted to see Spencer. I had to tell him about how I healed Wyatt, about not being able to heal Ariella, and ask him what did that mean.

I stopped by the dining room, which was filled with the scent of the most amazing food, and grabbed a nutmeg roll and a cup of faeberry juice. I would have eaten more, but I was too eager for that.

Just as I exited the dining room, Spencer walked out of the hospital wing. He smiled when he saw me. "Good morning. Slept well?"

My cheeks warmed with the memories of how Wyatt and I had *slept* in the back garden. Gods, I had been so turned on, I hadn't thought of anyone finding us at the time, but now I prayed we hadn't been seen. "Yup. Very well," I said with a smile.

The old fae nodded, then offered me a smile of his own. "Ready?"

I blinked. "For?"

He laughed. "I know you want to show me what you can do, and I want to help you with it."

I gaped at him. "How ... ?"

He waved his hand, dismissing my question. "Never mind that. Just come with me."

I followed him under the archway and found myself in an endless wide corridor, full of doors left and right. As we went, he pointed out things to me. The healers' room, where they met and talked and rested. The supply room. The triage area. The wide room with many beds where the patients with small injuries or not too sick stayed. Then the closed-off area where the private rooms and the people needing more attention were located.

Spencer first took me to see Ariella. As we walked into the larger room and dozens of beds lining the wall, he told me she was in a private room at first, because her wound had been too deep and she had lost a lot of blood. But they had been able to heal her and now she was in the shared room, since she was doing better and healing fast.

When we stopped beside her bed, Spencer lowered his voice as she was sleeping. I smiled, looking at her, thinking of the sentence "sleeping like an angel." She truly was an angel and she looked so at peace while sleeping. It was comforting.

"In another day or two, she should be able to move to the guests' wing with you," Spencer whispered.

A sense of relief bloomed in my chest. I had met Ariella not long ago, and we had had some rough patches in the beginning, but she had grown on me. Despite everything, I considered her a close friend and wanted what was best for her.

Next, Spencer took me to another bed in the same room, where a young female fae was seated, reading a thin leather bound book. She saw us stopping by her bedside and smiled at us.

"Good morning, Spencer," she said, her voice chipper.

He patted her blanket covered leg. "Morning, Marian. Feeling better?"

She nodded. "Oh, yes. It's almost fully healed."

He frowned. "Do you mind if we try something new?"

She gestured to her legs. "I trust you. Go ahead."

He pulled the edge of the blanket, uncovering her bare feet, and her lower legs, and folded the blankets on her knees. Ugly burn marks covered her fair skin. I inhaled suddenly.

"I want you to heal her," Spencer said, simply.

I stared at him. "Hm, what?"

"You won't be able to make the burn marks disappear right away, but you might be able to lessen them a little." He grabbed my wrists and placed my hands on her legs. The burn marks felt bumpy and cold to my touch. "Just relax and first think of the thing you love the most. Fill yourself with that feeling. *Then* push all that feeling into your new ability."

It sounded simple enough.

Inhaling deeply, I squared my shoulders and focused. The thing I loved the most? Not a thing. A person. A stubborn and hot tempered werewolf. My mate. Wyatt. I loved him with all my heart, all my soul, all my being.

When the feeling was too much and I thought my heart would burst, I transferred it forward, changing it to healing.

A tickling sensation covered my palms as my magic worked. Slowly, the burn marks became less red, less angry. I gasped, pulling my hand away.

"That's ... amazing," I whispered, in awe.

"Well done." Spencer smiled to Marian. "Thanks, my dear."

"Thank you," she said, looking at me, a genuine grin on her lips.

I nodded. Holding my elbow, Spencer steered me away from her bed. "The stronger the feeling, the more you'll be able to tap into it, and transform it into healing. With time and practice, you won't need to think as much, or focus as much. It'll have become instinct and you'll do it easily." He gestured to another bed, with an older male fae. "But for now, we practice on easier ones."

This fae had some stomachache. I was amazed I could help even with simple pain. For about two hours, I went around the room, healing one fae after another, but after all that, I felt drained.

When we left the common room, I sank into a chair in the healers' room.

"That too will change," Spencer assured me. "The more you practice it, the more you use your healing abilities, the less tired you'll feel." He sat down beside me. "But despite the exhaustion, how do you feel?"

I glanced down at my hands. "Stunned, amazed, alive." I faced him. "It's like I finally found my purpose in life." One that would be super short lived since I planned on sacrificing my life to the Bonecrown witches soon.

But for now, I would just enjoy it.

AFTER SOME REST, I CONTINUED WORKING WITH SPENCER all morning. At some point, Wyatt came looking for me, but seeing as I was aligned with this work, he simply placed a quick peck on my lips and told me to have fun.

I wouldn't call it fun, but it was very fulfilling.

Late morning, Spencer brought me a cup of faeberry juice. "You can stop anytime you want, you know."

I thanked him for the cup and took a long swallow. "I know, but I don't want to stop. Not yet. I'm just now understanding what to do. I want to learn more."

He chuckled. "Very well."

I emptied the cup, my mind shifting to another topic

that had been in my mind while I roamed this place. "Spencer, the fae realm is ruled by the shadow fae king, who is as evil as they come. How can this place be truly safe from him?" Often during the last few hours, I imagined the shadow fae soldiers marching in and taking everyone to the fae king's dungeons. If not killing everyone on sight.

"The shadow fae king knows better than to come here," he said, his tone flat, like I hadn't heard since I met him.

I opened my mouth to ask why, how could be so sure of that, but a blaze fae peeked into the room and called for his help with a patient. He excused himself and followed her into the hallway where all the private rooms were located.

I glanced at my empty cup and wondered if it would be too bad of me if I sneaked into the kitchens and grabbed some more of that yummy juice. Knowing I didn't have much to do here, and that I had already hidden for too many hours, I decided to go spend some time with Wyatt. Besides, now that Ariella was on the mend, we had to make plans. When we would go back. How we would take on the fae king. Did we have anything that might tip the scale to our side. Plans like those.

With my mind on that, I wandered out of the hospital wing and went in the direction of the guests' wing. Wyatt could be anywhere, but I could only think of our bedroom to check first.

I opened the door to our room, but he wasn't there. As I closed the door again, I hear a hiss followed by a string of curses. I stopped and listened for it. The cursing came again.

Recognizing that voice, I followed it, and ended up three doors down from mine. I knocked.

"Go away!" Corvina shouted. Then she let out another coarse hiss.

Something was wrong. With that in mind, I turned the knob and pushed the door open, thanking the stars she hadn't locked it. I stepped inside and found Corvina lying in bed, on her side, her black gown messy around her. She had droplets of sweat on her face, and her damp hair was plastered to her neck and shoulders.

"What happened?" I asked, walking to her.

She glared at me with bare teeth. "Get out!"

"Not until you tell me what's wrong."

She pressed a hand to her lower back and gritted her teeth, keeping a scream in. I leaned over her and placed my hands beside hers. I did what Spencer taught me—I thought of my love for Wyatt and let that guide me. When I directed that feeling into Corvina, it was strong and pure. It came into her like an avalanche, healing her from within.

She gasped as the pain lessened. I quickly found what was wrong—a defect in her lower spine. This bitch probably hurt like hell. How did she endure it? I kept focusing my powers into her, while I used my little knowledge of anatomy to fix her spine. I wasn't an expert, but I believed if I could just move it a little bit, it would already make all the difference for her.

Corvina clenched her teeth. I moved her spine and

healed the area around it. She let out another gasp and fell back on the bed, staring wide-eyed at the ceiling.

"How are you feeling?" I asked, afraid that I had messed it up and only made her feel worse.

Visibly exhausted, Corvina pushed up from the bed and bent forward, touching her fingertips to her toes. Then she bent her waist to one side, then the other.

"This is incredible," she whispered, looking at me, her dark eyes shining in wonder.

"Were you born with that defect?" I asked, hoping I didn't sound too nosey.

Nodding, she sat down on the bed. "Yes. It was always painful, and only got worse as I got older." She showed me a weak grin. "The other witches never knew. Can you imagine a powerful witch queen suffering from chronic back pain because of a defect? Instead, I just locked myself in my room and suffered through it in silence, pretending I was just in a bad mood and didn't want to see anyone."

"Now you won't have to pretend anymore. You can simply lock yourself because you want peace."

She chuckled. "I can't believe this." She touched her back again. "You shouldn't have done that, you know?"

I frowned. "Why not?"

"Because it won't change what I have to do with you once we get back." She swallowed hard. "To be honest, I don't approve of it, but there isn't much I can do about that. The previous queens set our power so the heart of the first witch queen needs sacrifices to keep it strong. Stronger than the other covens." She gazed at the floor. "During all these years, we've been sacrificing beings with weak powers, or no powers at all, but that just makes up for more killing."

I nodded, understanding. "If you sacrifice me, the heart won't need another one too soon."

"It would take at least ten years for us to have to do it again," she said, returning her gaze to me.

"I understand," I whispered. "It's a shame, because if you weren't destined to kill me, maybe we could even be friends."

She snorted, very un-queen-like. "Maybe."

I patted her shoulder. Before I made a fool of myself, I turned and walked out of the bedroom. There was no hope for me, so why bother with these talks?

Soon, I would die and I had to be okay with that.

12

WYATT

ONE THING I DIDN'T TELL FARRAH WAS HOW SICK I FELT after using my demon powers. The day after I found out about the demon wolf, I couldn't even get out of the fucking bed. I even threw up.

This was what Rey had warned me about, how this spell was temporary and would slowly claim my life.

As long as it lasted until this war was done and we defeated the shadow fae king … it was all that mattered.

Because of Ariella, we stayed in the castle for a few days, but Daleigh and Kayden had gone back to Earth, just to check on how things were going there. Hopefully, the fae king was quiet in his new and improved shadow castle, waiting for us to attack first.

But when Daleigh and Kayden came back, the news weren't good.

"His army is slowly pushing Luana's and Keeran's people back," Daleigh said, after we sat down around the dining table, in between meals. "If they keep pushing, I don't think they can hold on much longer."

"We need to go back," Kayden added. "We need to go help, but more than that, we need a plan to defeat him. Just marching in there and fighting might not be the way."

Seated beside me, Farrah frowned. "Then what is the way?"

Kayden shrugged. "I don't know, but from the looks of it, the wolves, warlocks, and the frost fae we left there might not be enough. We need a larger number."

"Could you call the blaze fae?" I asked.

Kayden turned her amber eyes to me. "I can, but that wasn't our deal. My father might not allow them to come."

I shrugged. "There's only one way of knowing." I was going to say more, but I heard a new sound coming a mile away. "Wait. I hear something." I strained my ears, trying to make sense of the sound. I got up and followed it to the front door of the castle, then inhaled deeply, trying to get a scent to go with the sound. It was faint, but I felt it. "There are many fae coming this way."

"What?" Farrah asked, her eyes wide. "To attack us?"

I shook my head. "No. From the scent, I think they are hurt."

"Fugitives," Corvina whispered. She had been a shadow around us, but now she had a fierce gleam in her dark eyes.

"I'll go warn Spencer," Daleigh said a second before turning and running into the hospital wing.

Meanwhile, Farrah, Kayden, Corvina, and I dashed across the front garden to help them. I thought I was prepared for them, since I could smell them and tell how many they were, but I still inhaled a sharp breath and anger boiled into me at their sight. Dozens of fae emerged from the forest, with bloodied arms, chests, and head. Some were being carried in fae's arms, or even in stretchers.

"What happened?" I asked, picking up an old female fae who almost face planted on the ground.

"The shadow fae king," a male fae said. "He sent his troops to our village. We don't know why."

My anger increased. Because he was evil, I wanted to say, but I kept that in. I kept my mouth shut and helped the fae to the hospital.

A moment later, Daleigh was back with Spencer and other healer fae, and we all helped them into the castle. The most critical ones went directly to private rooms, or now shared ones since there wasn't a room for everyone. The others waited their turn in the common rooms. The uninjured ones, but visible shaken, were spread out around the dining, sitting, and the foyer. Farrah had disappeared with the other healers, ready to help.

Kayden and Daleigh went around the room, handing out water they had gathered from the kitchen, while I walked around, making sure everyone was okay—as okay as they could be in this situation. Even Corvina helped, doing the same thing as me.

Hours passed in a flurry of movement and sadness. Some lives were lost, but most injured fae would recover, Spencer announced. But from what they mentioned, the fae king army wasn't done. After razing through their village, the army marched out in the direction of another.

What the fuck was the fae king doing, wiping out the entire fae race? He would be king of what then? Air? Dirt?

It didn't make sense. But evil rarely did.

It was only a matter of time before more fae appeared and the castle was inundated. It could barely hold on as it was.

We needed to defeat the fae king *now*.

A couple more hours passed and things seemed to settle down in a new, crazy rhythm. At least, there had been no new arrivals and the injured fae was now on the mend. It seemed we could take a deep breath now, so I called on my friends. Farrah, Daleigh, Kayden, Corvina, and even Ariella came to meet me in the back porch, which seemed to be the only place where the fae hadn't spread out to yet.

Ariella was still a little paler than usual, and her movements were a little slower, but other than that, she looked good. Ready for a fight.

"We need to go," I started the conversation. "The longer we take to kill the fae king, the worse it'll be. Luana and Keeran can't hold him out for long, and Spencer and the other healers can't heal and house the entire fae realm."

"You're right," Kayden said. "Actually, during a quick breather this morning, I sent word to the blaze fae in the human realm. If they decide to help, they will be on their way to the shadow fae king's new castle now."

"Good." I nodded. "But you all know it might not be enough, right?"

"What if we do like we need with the frost fae before?" Daleigh suggested. "Let's ask around here who wants to join us. Even if we can get half a dozen able fae who is willing to fight, it's better than nothing."

"We should ask them," Ariella said. "Just make sure they know what they are getting into. Unfortunately, many will lose their lives in this fight."

Farrah let out a long sigh. "It's sad, but it's true." She shook her head. "I wish there was another way."

I hooked my arm around her waist. "Me too."

Corvina snickered. "I agree, but count me out of talking to them. Just tell me when you're all ready and let's go." She walked away from us, but from what Farrah had told me, the ice around the witch queen's heart was melting. Maybe by the end of this mess, she would take pity on Farrah and let me take her place in the sacrifice, even if my powers weren't as strong.

"All right," Kayden said, her voice deep, like the leader she was supposed to be. "Let's talk to the fae and see who wants to join us."

"When are we leaving?" Daleigh asked.

Kayden glanced up at the sky. "It's getting dark soon, and these people are obviously tired. Let them rest tonight." Her shoulders relaxed. "We should rest too. We leave tomorrow morning, before sunrise."

We all agreed and set out to convince fae to fight and die with us.

13

FARRAH

WYATT, DALEIGH, ARIELLA, AND KAYDEN WENT TO TALK TO the other fae to see who was up to join us, Corvina disappeared, and I went back to the hospital, to see how I could help before I left tomorrow.

I would be sad about leaving this place, but we couldn't hide in here forever. It was clear the fae king wouldn't stop harassing his own people and the people on Earth, if given the chance. I was damn tired of battles and deaths, but I would make an exception for him.

I couldn't wait to see him dead.

It was late at night when I returned to my bedroom in the guests' wing. But Wyatt wasn't here. I followed my instincts and went to the back of the castle, where I had found him that first night.

As I expected it, there he was, alone and practicing his new powers. I still couldn't believe he had somehow stolen Drollmor's magic and was now very powerful, maybe even more powerful than me? We hadn't put that to the test yet.

With his hearing and scent, he knew I was watching him from a small distance, but he kept practicing, enveloping his arms in dark flames, then shooting them at improvised targets in front of trees.

After two quick rounds, Wyatt groaned and doubled over.

My chest tightened and I ran to him. I held him before he face planted on the ground, but we only fell together, with me softening some of his fall.

"What's wrong?" I asked, my voice frantic.

Wyatt stirred with his back on top of my legs, his hands pressed to his stomach. His forehead was clammy with sweat droplets and his teeth were gritted. On instinct, I placed my hands over his body and used my newfound healing abilities to find what was wrong.

I inhaled deeply as I found out there was everything wrong. His body was practically shutting down. I pushed my magic into him, stopping him from dying right here, right now.

After a long time, when I was sure he wouldn't die, I withdrew my power. Slowly, Wyatt's breathing went back to normal. He looked at me, a sadness covering his eyes.

"What the hell was that?" I asked.

14

WYATT

I DIDN'T WANT FARRAH TO FIND OUT I WAS FUCKING DYING, not yet. But she had just healed me, probably kept me from throwing my guts out, and enduring much more pain. My mind spun, trying to come up with some lie, but I couldn't lie to her anymore.

"There was a price to stealing Drollmor's powers." I sat up but stayed close to her. "I'll be very powerful, but eventually, it'll kill me."

Her face became white. "W-what? Why would you do something like that?"

"Because!" I started shouting, but inhaled deeply, calming myself down. There was no reason for me to be mad right now. She would be pissed at me, but what was done, was done. "I talked to Corvina and tried exchanging your life for mine. She said she needs someone powerful and you're the most powerful from all of us. Or was. Once I stole Drollmor's magic, I became powerful too, I just don't know if it's enough." It had to be. I had to make sure

Corvina accepted me this way. "Hopefully, Corvina will take me in your place now."

She stared at me for a long time, her mind working through this mess. "So, either way now, you're dying."

I nodded. "You have to understand, Farrah. I love you way too much. I would die a million times over to save you from anything. If I can't live without you, then let me die." I gestured to the castle behind us. "You found your calling. After we defeat the fae king and I give myself to the Bonecrown witches, you can come here and fulfill a purpose." I reached over and held her hand in mine. "If you die and leave me alone, I'll be lost. I'll probably just kill myself. It'll serve no one."

"No." She shook her head. "I can't believe you did that." Her eyes softened, shining with unshed tears. "You're so stupid."

"A stupid in love," I said, trying a small smile.

She hooked her arm around my shoulders and pulled me closer to her. "I should be mad at you right now. Well, I am, in a way. But I also know that our time is limited and I won't waste it by fighting with you."

I let out a long, relieved breath. I rested my forehead on hers. "Then let's *not* fight." I brushed my lips on hers and she shivered. In one swift movement, I hooked my arm around her waist, twisted us around, placed her on the soft grass, and lay down over her. "I think we better get to our bedroom before we do a repeat of the other night right here."

She hooked her legs around my waist, grounding her hips against mine. "Just because there are more fae in the castle now? I bet they will be very entertained watching us."

I chuckled, but when she pressed her feet on my ass again, rubbing her hips on mine, I groaned. There was no fighting with her, that was for sure. All I wanted to do was sink into her, melt into her, bury myself so deep into her that nothing would ever be able to pry us apart.

I captured her mouth with mine, my lips demanding and my tongue urgent. She was mine, all mine, and I needed her right now.

A boom echoed through the silent night, followed by the shaking of the ground. I pushed away from Farrah and looked out to the castle. Shouts came from inside. I grabbed Farrah's hand in mine and shot up, pulling her with me.

"What the hell?" she asked, her voice low.

I pressed my lips tight. "I think we're under attack."

15

Wyatt and I scurried to join the others in the castle. A line of healer fae were already outside, fighting back a horde of shadow fae soldiers who were trying to break through.

What the hell?

Kayden and Ariella were among the first fae to join the fight. Daleigh came rushing from the guests' wing, and Corvina appeared from whatever corner she had been hiding.

"What's going on?" she asked, glancing around at the running fae. Her gaze settled to the open entrance and the shadow fae beyond. "What the fuck? Are hospitals a sacred place during wars or something like that?"

"Apparently not on this war," Wyatt muttered. He nudged my arm. "Let's go."

The four of us joined the others and fought the shadow fae, trying to keep them back. They threw shadow bombs over us, toward the castle, rattling walls and hitting other fae.

More soldiers came from the sides and we had to spread thin. Kayden used her fire, Daleigh cast frost spells, Ariella used her light powers, Corvina threw shadow bolts, and Wyatt transformed into his new demon wolf.

And I rose ice soldiers from nothing and sent them to attack the shadow fae soldiers.

A few fae from our side were hit and went back to the hospital. A few lost their lives at our feet. Here and there, a soldier sneaked past us and made it back to the castle. They were quickly stopped after, but until then, they had cut through a few other fae, and thrown another shadow bomb inside the hospital.

I didn't even want to see how bad the casualties would be after this.

But we were succeeding. The shadow fae was dying at our hands, and the remaining ones were being pushed back.

Hours seemed to pass and we were all tired and sweating, almost drained from all our powers, when finally, the few shadow fae soldiers still alive ran for it.

It was well past midnight when we sank at the front stairs of the castle, unable to lift another muscle.

A set of heavy footsteps came from behind us and an enraged Spencer stomped out the door. I had never seen such a fierce look on his eyes.

"That is it," he announced, his voice sharp. "I changed my mind. I won't just sit here and be neutral about it when that forsaken shadow fae king isn't. I'm taking this fight to him."

I gaped at him. "You'll join us in fighting him?"

"I will." He paused. "But not right away." He glanced around to all of us. My friends and his, all tired and dirty. "Take a couple of hours to clean up and rest. Leave before the sun rises. I'll meet you at his new castle later. I promise."

With that, he marched inside the castle again.

"As much as I would love to go kick the shadow fae king right now, I think he's right," Kayden said. "We need to rest."

"Agreed," Daleigh said, nodding his head. "Meet back here before sunrise?"

"Yes. And don't forget to tell the others we had recruit to join us," Ariella said. "I just hope this attack gave them more purpose and didn't scare them into hiding."

They pushed up and walked away, to warn the other fae and rest.

Wyatt tugged me closer to him. "Shall we go rest?"

"I'm not sure I can get up from here," I told him, and it was the truth. I was so damn tired. Despite all the exhaustion, part of me wanted to get up and go check on the fae at the hospital and make sure they were all right. Help where I could. But Spencer was right. I had to fight tomorrow, and for that, I needed rest. "Carry me?"

Wyatt chuckled, but despite being as dead as I felt, he shot up, holding me in his arms. "Always."

16

WYATT

IT WAS STILL DARK WHEN SEVERAL PORTALS WERE OPENED and we crossed them over to the human realm. Since we didn't know exactly where Luana and Keeran and their army were right now, we portaled to a nearby road, from where we marched toward the new shadow fae castle.

We found them halfway to the castle—almost half a mile back from where we left them. They had set up temporary tents from where the supernaturals rested, ate, and were treated if wounded, and in the distance, the fighting raged on. Werewolves, warlocks, and frost fae against the shadow fae soldiers. While we had been out, it seemed Thea had sent witches and Drake had sent vampires to help out.

As we spread out to check on their progress, to help with the wounded, to find Luana and Keeran, who apparently were deep into the fray, the Blaze fae arrived. They greeted Kayden with respect, like a real leader.

Like a queen.

Once we defeated the shadow fae king, Kayden would become queen. And I was confident she would be much, much better than him.

What I wasn't too confident about, though, was if we would really defeat the fae king. When I looked around, everything was a mess, and more wounded fae came back from the front lines, sometimes carrying the dead body of a friend.

It fucking hurt to watch.

Sometime past noon, Luana and Keeran came back to the tents, both of them bloody and sweating and plain dirty. They sank into chairs in the main tent and drank tons of waters while their right and left hands reported about advancements, injuries, casualties, and the arrival of more allies.

Luana shook her head. "Thank goodness you're all here. I'm not sure we would have lasted another day like this." She glanced at Kayden. "With your people and the fae who came with you, we might just a chance."

"True," Keeran said, washing his hands in a basin over a corner table. "But just standing there and fighting them won't be enough. We need a plan."

Farrah was the one who spoke next. "I might have a plan."

BEFORE SUNSET, WE MADE OUR WAY AROUND THE SIDES OF the castle, but stayed concealed by the thick lines of trees in the forest. When it was dark, we advanced. Here, there were only a few soldiers probably because the main action was still being played at the front of the castle—but not for long.

The frost and the blaze fae lead the groups, either burning the shadow fae soldiers alive or freezing them over. And we moved toward the castle.

Farrah's plan was to have everyone fight to get us inside —her, Daleigh, Luana, Keeran, Ariella, Kayden, Corvina, and I. If more people made it inside, great, but if they didn't, they had to keep the soldiers out, engaged into battle or killed. It was the only way because if we had to fight the soldiers *and* the fae king, we would certainly lose.

But the eight of us might have a chance.

As we crept up toward the castle, I felt something brush against my ankle. I was about to kick it when I saw it was Rusty. What the fuck was that cat doing here?

Who cared? As long as he stayed away from the fight, I was fine with it.

We had to cross one of the few bridges over the pit filled with black water, then fight a few soldiers guarding one of the side entrances, but with all of us, it wasn't hard at all. In no time, we were inside the castle.

But it was nothing like we expected.

The walls, the corridors, the rooms—they were all gone.

The castle was just a thick outer black glass wall, shining like a million of stars, and nothing else. The interior was one endless room.

And right in the center stood the shadow fae king.

Waiting for us.

17

FARRAH

THIS HAD BEEN A TRAP.

All along, the fae king had just stood here, waiting for us.

And we had come to him, like dazed moths.

We took a few steps into the cavernous room, where the fae king stood alone. Slowly, he turned around, a lazy grin spreading over his lips. I winced, appalled at how he reminded of his son. Prince Lark had been an exact copy of his father, just younger.

"My dear Farrah," he said, his voice echoing in the distant walls. I winced again. Even that was just like Prince Lark. "I'm finally meeting my daughter-in-law."

"I'm not that anymore," I rasped through my gritted teeth.

"Oh, I know." His eyes darkened, the shadows around him moving. Alive. "You killed my beloved son." He tsked. "I was very disappointed in you, Farrah. From all I had heard about you, I really liked you. Well, I still like you, and that's why I'll make a deal with you."

I scoffed. "I'm not making any more deals in this lifetime."

He ignored me and went on. "If you surrender to me, I won't harm you. You'll live like a recluse guest in my palace. A luxurious prisoner, if you will."

I frowned. "And—?"

"That's it." He shook his head once, as if puzzled. "I will kill your friends anyway. The deal is for you: die in this very room, or live a fancy life at my castle."

I gaped at him. Did he think I was that stupid? I would take a million deaths before being his silly princess locked in a tower.

"Go to hell," I said.

"I'm already in it." He threw his hand at me and the shadows jetted to me.

Just then, Rusty, who had suddenly joined us when we were entering the castle, jumped from the floor, becoming ten times bigger than he was before, with sharp teeth and ferocious eyes. Rusty took the brunt of the spell, but somehow, he absorbed most of it.

I gasped, stunned by his abilities. I had heard of how feline fae were magical in ways the fae weren't, but I had never heard about that!

Beside me, Wyatt groaned. He transformed into his demon wolf and lunged toward the king. All of my friends did.

But they never got too close.

Shadow cages rose from the shiny black floor, trapping them all inside, each of them alone. Even Rusty was taken.

I faced the fae king.

"Let them go!" I screamed.

"It doesn't work that way," he said, walking toward me with slow, deliberate steps. "Just give up, my dear Farrah. Give in. You aren't a match for me."

I slipped my hand in the pocket of my pants and closed my palm around the Frost Pendant. I channeled the power in it. I might not have been a match for him before, but now ... even if I still wasn't, I had to try.

I rose my hand and erected a wall of ice around it. A second later, it exploded in a million pieces the shards flying out like daggers. Two of them scratched my shoulder and arms, drawing a thin line of blood.

Enough playing. Focusing, I summoned my frost soldiers. A dozen of them surrounded the fae king, with me standing beside them. In synchrony, we threw frost magic at the fae king. I gritted my teeth, pouring every ounce of power I had in my veins into the jet flying out of my hands.

For a moment, the fae king was enveloped in white, my frost covering every inch of him. But just like before, he simply shook off, like a dog shaking water from its fur, and the frost melted like a big puddle at his feet.

Then he lifted his hand and a wave of shadow coursed through the room. My warriors disappeared almost instantly. The wave hit me in the chest, robbing me of air and throwing me several feet back. I fell on the dark floor, heaving as if I had run a marathon.

The shadow fae king loomed over me and smiled as he drained the magic from me. "Now, my dear Farrah, you meet your end."

18

WYATT

I POUNCED ON THE WALLS OF THE SHADOW CAGE, MY muscles screaming at me at the effort, but that pain was nothing compared to the way my insides twisted while I watched the fae king hover over to Farrah.

With her head down and her shoulders sagged, she looked so little, so fragile, so weak. So exhausted. This way, she wouldn't be able to fight him, much less defeat him.

I stopped for a second, trying to think. I had seen Farrah summon ice soldiers all the time, she had just done that, but that was one spell I hadn't tried yet. Still in my wolf form, I focused and used my magic to summon shadowy forms. Though, it didn't go as I had planned. Instead of shadowy forms, dozens of minor demons appeared inside and outside the cage—all of them real.

The ones outside flew to the fae king, while the ones inside with me used their strength and borrowed magic to push against the shadow walls.

I took half a second to marvel at the extent of Droll-mor's powers before acting. I pushed along with the demons howling as my muscles burned on the inside. Suddenly, the shadow cage exploded in a swirl of smoke and I fell on the hard stone floor.

I ignored the pain, the moment, and sent the rest of the demons to the fae king. I shifted back to my human form and ran to Farrah. I crouched beside her just as her body slumped. I caught her before her head hit the floor.

"Farrah." I held her closer to me. "Talk to me. Are you okay?"

She blinked, finally seeing me. "I'm ... tired." She groaned, sitting up. "But I'll live. For now."

We turned our heads to the fae king.

As if there were bugs around him, he swung his hand out to sweep them off. A dark wave washed over the room. It touched the lesser demons and their forms broke off into ashes.

The shadow fae king locked his eyes at Farrah and me, his lips tugging up. "You can't win."

He opened his hands wide and the room shook. A loud groan bounced over the walls as the floor cracked and crumbled, forming a wide, depthless ring around Farrah and me.

Holding hands, Farrah and I stood. If the floor cracked just a tiny bit more, the two of us would go tumbling down into the infinite darkness.

"We can't jump that wide," she said, her voice low.

No, we couldn't. Maybe I could if I transformed into my

demon wolf and I could take her with me, but then what? It was clear we wouldn't be able to kill the fae king by ourselves.

There was no way out.

19

FARRAH

THIS WASN'T SUPPOSED TO BE THE WAY WE DIED, BUT I couldn't think of a way out. Our friends were all inside the shadow cages, and Wyatt and I were trapped in a fragile ledge in the middle of a chasm.

The fae king had won.

Fear clutched my chest as I turned to Wyatt. "He'll kill us."

"I know," he muttered. His hands found my waist and he pulled me to him, holding me tight. "I love you, Farrah. Much more than you can imagine."

My heart swelled. "No more than I love you."

I grabbed on to his shoulders as if they were my anchors. "I hope we find each other again one day." I glanced up into his hazel eyes. "Mates forever."

He leaned into me. "Mates forever." He brushed his lips against mine, a soft and warm sensation, so unlike the cold pit of despair growing in my stomach.

Suddenly, the doors to the room burst open, letting in light and a gust of chilly wind.

Spencer marched into the room, long white robes flowing behind him.

The fae king balked. "What are *you* doing here?"

"This is enough," Spencer barked. His voice, the frown on his face. I had never seen him this mad before. This angry. "I've tried to remain neutral through all of this, but you have gone too far."

I watched, stunned. What the hell he was talking about?

White light surrounded Spencer and his features changed slightly. His hair grew longer, his wrinkles smoothed a little, his back hunch straightened, and he gained an inch or two in height.

I gasped. I had seen him before, pictures and drawings of him in books.

"The Father of all Fae," I whispered, in shock.

"Yield," Spencer said, his voice cutting through the air like a sword.

"Never!" the fae king shouted.

"So be it." Spencer threw out his hands—one wave of white light rolled over Wyatt and me, enveloping us and shielding us from the rays of light raging against the shadow fae king.

The king used his own shadow magic against Spencer, but even he wasn't that powerful. More white light flashed, blinding us for a moment.

When we were able to open our eyes again, I just stared, rooted in place.

The floor was whole again, the cages were gone, my brother and friends released, and right in the center of the room stood Spencer, watching over the fallen body at his feet.

The shadow fae king had been defeated.

Spencer turned to Wyatt and me. "This isn't over yet." He flew out of the room—literally flew, his feet not touching the floor—and went outside.

We heard some yells and small explosions, but soon, everything went quiet.

"What the hell was that?" Ariella asked, her gaze shifting to the body on the floor. "Is he really dead?"

"That was the Father of all Fae," Kayden said, her quiet tone indicating she was as in much shock as I was. "The most powerful fae of all."

Daleigh took a step closer to the body and poked it with the tip of his boot. "I thought that was just a legend. Or better, that he was long gone from our world."

"Me too," I whispered. How could the Father of All Fae be right beside us all this time and we had no idea?

"Well, at least he showed up," Corvina said. She glanced at her long, black nails as if this was all too boring for her. "Speaking of showing up." She stared at the doors.

Romulus, Meira, Aspen, Boise, Myra, and others started filling the room, to check on us, and to know what happened.

"A fae stormed outside and annihilated the shadow fae soldiers," Myra said, sounding slightly amazed for a supposedly cold-hearted witch.

"It was unexpected," Romulus said.

Meira nodded. "And amazing."

"Where is he now?" I asked, glancing around and looking for him. I had questions for him ... why hadn't he interfered before? If he had this much power, why hadn't he killed the shadow fae king long ago and restored everything to normal?

They shrugged.

"He just vanished," Aspen said.

"All right, I think this is enough standing around," Kayden said, taking over. "We need to dispose of the bodies and help the injured."

Wyatt nodded. "She's right."

"Let's do this," Ariella agreed.

We moved out, knowing we had a lot of work to do.

20

WYATT

For the next couple of hours, we helped the injured, cleared the dead, and buried the fallen shadow king. Even if he was a fucking bastard, he got a marked grave.

As we worked, and moved, and got things done, my muscles contracted, and pain ricocheted through me. The effects of stealing Drollmor's powers. I didn't have much time left.

After, when the sun was rising again, we met at the entrance of the Starlight Vale, but Corvina, Myra, and other Bonecrown witches halted in Farrah's way.

"It's time," Corvina said, her eyes downcast, her lip pressed into a thin line. I had seen how she had come to respect Farrah and how this hurt her.

It hurt me too.

"I'll do it," I said out loud. Everyone turned to me—Luana, Keeran, Ariella, Daleigh, Kayden, and the witches. I stared at Corvina. "I'm more powerful than the last time we talked."

She nodded, holding my gaze. "I know. I also know you're dying."

I frowned. How did she know that? I had only told Farrah about it. Could she sense it? "Then just do it. Since I'm dying, use me as a sacrifice. And leave Farrah alone."

Farrah grabbed my arm. "Wyatt ..."

We already had this conversation. I wouldn't change my mind now. I gasped and doubled over as a wave of pain rolled over my stomach. I sank to the ground, Farrah by my side.

The Bonecrown witches formed a circle around us.

"Wait, no." Luana pushed through the circle. "There has to be another way."

"You heard him." Corvina glanced at Luana. "He's dying. I'm just making his death useful."

"But—"

"It was my choice, Luana," I told her, my voice strained. "I'm taking Farrah's place. It's my decision. You would have done the same for Keeran."

She held my gaze for a breath, then nodded. Her lips turned upside down, she stepped back.

I groaned as the pit in my stomach grew. Farrah held on to me tighter.

"It's okay," I whispered, the muscles in my arms weakening. "Just remember I love you."

She swallowed a gasp. "I love you too."

"Farrah," Corvina said.

Slowly, Farrah retreated, but she never took her eyes from mine. I wanted to be strong enough not to look at her while this happened, but I couldn't. If these were my last moments on this Earth, I wanted to spend them by drinking her in as much as I could.

The witches' chanting echoed around me, their magic brushing against my skin, but all I saw, all I knew was Farrah. Her pretty, delicate rose lips. Her fair, smooth skin. Her long, silver white hair. Her contagious smile. Her big heart.

I love you, my dear mate.

My strength vanished and I crumbled, falling on the ground, my back crushing the grass below me.

I snapped my head to the side, so I could keep looking at Farrah, but my vision blurred, the shadows growing thick on the corner of my eyes. My breath became shallow and my power left me inch by inch.

Then nothing.

I was nothing. Dead. I was sure I was dead.

A bright white glob hovered over me.

An angel? Heaven? After all the fucking things I had done in this life? I didn't deserve going to heaven.

"What's that?"

It was Farrah.

Suddenly awake, I sat up. I frowned. What the fuck was happening?

"It's his powers," Corvina said. "The ones he stole from the higher demon." Her eyes turned all black and she consumed the powers, probably to finish the ceremony in her coven later. She needed to pass that power to the heart of the first witch queen, otherwise all of this was for nothing.

I patted down my chest. "I'm alive? I don't understand."

"It seems our sacrifice ceremony just took the powers you stole from Drollmor," Corvina explained. "If that happened, then it should be enough. And you'll remain living."

Farrah pulled down the neck of her shirt and looked at her shoulder. No more marks of the blood pact. She gasped. "No sacrifices, then? From him or me?"

Corvina shook her head. "No, no more sacrifices."

With a squeal, Farrah threw herself over me. I barely managed to lift my arms and catch her before the two of us hit the ground and broke something. She wrapped her arms around my shoulders and squeezed hard.

"You're here."

I held her to me. "I've got another chance at this thing called life and I'm not wasting it." I kissed the top of her head. "I'm not letting go of you ever again."

"I'm counting on it." She slipped her hands up my neck and planted her lips on mine.

Groans reached our ears, but we ignored them. If people didn't want to see me ravishing my mate right here and right now, they should walk away.

21

FARRAH

I DIPPED MY TOES IN THE WATER AND INHALED DEEPLY, THE salty air filling my lungs. Behind me, the sun was setting, and the moon and the stars dotted the sky above the sea.

I glanced back, at the cottage several yards back, just out of the range of the sand, the small wooden building standing out among so many tall trees.

A smile crept into my lips as Wyatt moved around the wraparound porch, pushing the furniture around.

It had taken a long road for us to get here, but we had done it.

After the battle at the shadow castle, the clean up, and the Bonecrown witches' sacrifice, Corvina promised she would find another way to deal with the sacrifices, even if she had to kill a bunch of cockroaches and spiders per day to make up for it. Whatever it took.

Keeran and Luana left soon after, taking their warlocks and werewolves with them. The vampires and witches who had been sent by Drake and Thea also left.

Spencer had come and explained his plans for the fae realm: he proclaimed Kayden the rightful heir of the fae realm's throne. She took over the mantle with honor, promising to be fair and respectful. She abolished the curse not allowing fae to fall in love with other supernaturals or humans, and to allow them to be brought over to the fae realm.

She also appointed Daleigh as the Lord of the frost court, to rule over the frost fae, since now my kind was again a part of that world.

Ariella had left without a goodbye. It reminded me of when Wyatt and I disappeared from Luana's and Keeran's lives. We hadn't meant for it to hurt them, but now I knew how they had felt. Despite our rough beginning, Ariella had become a good friend, and now she had simply walked away.

I just hoped she found what she was looking for and our paths crossed again.

Though she would have to come this way, because I wasn't leaving this place ever again.

After Kayden and Daleigh had escorted the fae back to the fae realm, Spencer had invited me to go back with them. I couldn't, not with Wyatt in the human realm. He could come with me now, I knew that, but I also knew we didn't belong there. So, he blessed me with a powerful spell that wouldn't allow me to grow weak and die in the human realm. I would live as a normal fae even if I stayed here forever.

He also appointed me an ambassador for the fae realm. Should the need arise, I would act as a mediator between the fae and the human realms. I really hoped the need never came, because after Wyatt and I found this destroyed cottage at the beachside, away from any town or civilization, and we had worked for weeks to restore it and give it a semblance of a real home, I wasn't willing to go anywhere.

Finally, Wyatt put down the long chaise, stepped back, and admired his work. I chuckled under my breath, knowing that tomorrow he would wake up thinking the chair would look better on the other side again.

With an easy grin, he walked over to me. He placed a possessive arm around my shoulders and pulled me closer.

"What are you looking at?" he asked, his voice soft.

I sighed. "At you. At our little home. At the ocean and the night sky." I rested the side of my head on his shoulder. "I like it here. I like you."

He laughed. "And I like you. Fuck, no. I love you."

I glanced up at him. We had gone through so much before, almost lost each other so many times, I didn't even like to remember. But here we were. Together, as we should have been from the start.

"I love you too," I whispered.

This time, it would be forever.

THANK YOU

Thank you for reading *The Blood Pact*!

Reviews are very important for authors. If you liked my book, please consider leaving a review on your favorite retailer and/or on goodreads, please!

Did you like this book? You can check out other books of mine:

The Demon Kiss (Rite World: Blackthorn Hunters Academy book 1): a fast-paced story about a young woman who finds out she's a demon hunter, and the half-demon intent on protecting her against all evil.

The Vampire Heir (Rite World 1: Rite of the Vampire): a dark and mysterious paranormal romance about a vampire and a young woman with a secret.

The Warlock Lord (Rite World 4: Rite of the Warlock): a thrilling and kick-ass paranormal romance about a werewolf and warlock.

Heart Seeker (The Fire Heart Chronicles book 1): an

urban fantasy series about a young woman who finds herself at the center of a mysterious supernatural world.

Destiny Gift (The Everlast Series book 1): a post-apocalyptic urban fantasy series about a young woman with a special power that can save the world.

Don't forget to sign up for my Newsletter to find out about new releases, cover reveals, giveaways, and more!

If you want to see exclusive teasers, help me decide on covers, read excerpts, talk about books, etc, join my reader group on Facebook: Juliana's Club!

ABOUT THE AUTHOR

While USA Today Bestselling Author Juliana Haygert dreams of being Wonder Woman, Buffy, or a blood elf shadow priest, she settles for the less exciting—but equally gratifying—life as a wife, a mother, and an author. She resides in North Carolina and spends her days writing about kick-ass heroines and the heroes who drive them crazy.

Subscribe to her mailing list to receive emails of announcement, events, and other fun stuff related to her writing and her books: www.bit.ly/JuHNL

For more information:
www.julianahaygert.com

facebook.com/julianahaygert

twitter.com/juliana_haygert

instagram.com/juliana.haygert

goodreads.com/juliana_haygert

pinterest.com/julianahaygert

bookbub.com/authors/juliana-haygert

ALSO BY JULIANA HAYGERT

To find links and more info, go to:

www.julianahaygert.com/books/

Shorts

Into the Darkest Fire

Tested

Rite World: Blackthorn Hunters Academy

The Demon Kiss (Book 1)

The Hunter Secret (Book 2)

The Soul Bond (Book 3)

The Shadow Trials (Book 4)

The Infernal Curse (Book 5)

Rite World

The Vampire Heir (Book 1)

The Witch Queen (Book 2)

The Immortal Vow (Book 3)

The Warlock Lord (Book 4)

The Wolf Consort (Book 5)

The Crystal Rose (Book 6)

The Wolf Forsaken (Book 7)

Siren's Song (Book 5)

www.ingramcontent.com/pod-product-compliance
Lightning Source LLC
Chambersburg PA
CBHW021738190726
48288CB00009B/3099